My Heart

A poetry collection of loss, depression, hurt, longing, admiration and thoughts.

NICOLE YATES

ISBN: 978-1-7635589-0-8
First edition, 2024

Cover illustration by Brodie M Condon

For book orders and enquiries, contact:
Email: nicole.yates94@gmail.com

A catalogue record for this book is available from the National Library of Australia

Contents

Dedication

To my family, my friends
(you know who you are my dear nakama),
my twin flame, and those whose music
helped me through tough times
(Joan and Stefani).

I write from my heart.
For those who read this may
it resonate with your heart too.

Loss

Mourning Ode

Tears fall into the ocean,
Screaming your absence,
Death your defence.

As I sit on my fence,
Teetering between life,
Teetering between death,
I choose what is best.

Life is like a tear drop,
Death is like opening a door to a space,
Before eternal life anticipate,
Weighing of your deeds,
Which sow the seeds,
For your eternity.

Smile in that spirits domain,
For it is free from pain,
May the living remember your name.

Breeze

Like a breeze, you left,
Pain and tears all that's left,
Memory is brief like your time with me,
How could a disease so cruel take you from me?

Hollow like a hole,
Wanting to feel whole,
Missing your family role,
Wondering what if?

What if you're with me in spirit?
Wholeness in my spirit,
To know in some manner,
That I matter; to you.

Loss

Unbearable pain,
Love heals not in vain,
Your soul reflecting in my tears,
All of our together years.

Pain like time slowly flows,
Pain ebbs on certain days,
Missing you in the photo frame,
Alas, the reaper is to blame.

I try to speak, your name,
My voice trembles; meek,
Waiting for the day we meet,
Time numbs pain.

Without End

Ripped from my heart,
Two realms apart,
Time aches on ahead,
Rather be with you instead.

You're without physical shape,
Your spirit takes its place,
There is no meeting space,
Life is not a race.

Nor, is death final,
Hope is for revival,
For when we meet again,
Time will be without end.

Dismantled

Dismantled like a toy falling apart,
Your parting glass the last,
Sobs; echoed that day,
There is pain in parting ways,
Oh, life dismantled like tragedy unraveling.

Yet, you gifted, me; hope,
Now isn't the time to choke,
A toy made of glass,
Can be repaired in parts,
Only, slowly and in the heart.

Time you do not mask,
Oh, healing from grieving,
Now rest, dear spirit!

Memory

How can one grasp your memory,
When this one has trouble with memory,
Photos and videos refresh what was,
Photos and videos refresh what's lost.

Why is this one's brain cruel?
Why is this one's brain cruel to you?
Love! Is the only thing the brain can't rob!
Even, when there is memory fog.

Weep to Seek

I weep as the reaper took you,
I weep as no one can replace you,
I weep as your love is hard to beat.

I seek the Divine's healing,
I seek my heart mending,
I seek your never ending love,
I seek wisdom from above.

Smile

You pass your smile down the generations,
Life with your laughter was sweet,
Life without your laughter is bitter,
Though, I know your smile is still here with us.

In those gentle creases of dimples,
Like yours; reflect on mine,
I see your smile in the mirror,
Your smile stays with us forever.

Down the generations your smile will go,
That smile of yours will still grow,
Long till the end of time,
Your smile will be reflected in mine!

Joker

When that joker told his jokes,
Laughter would be evoked,
These are the golden memories,
That diagnosis; that horrible word.

Both our worlds crumbled,
Cancer like a thief stole you from us,
Yet, cancer cannot take your love of and for us,
Remembered always with a smile,

Joker; laugh, it's good for the soul.

Depression

Cloak of Sadness

Here I wear my cloak of sadness,
The bitterness of others,
Cause myself to wear it.

It makes me sink into the abyss,
With no words of kindness,
Mind the sadness.

Its heavy and no one notices,
Perhaps its too dark to see,
The cloak of sadness around me.

Under the Wave

Under the wave I go again,
Back onto the ocean floor,
Where I wont feel anymore,
To where hurt can't touch me.

Yet, it is because of hurt,
Why do I try?
For the feeling of happiness,
For the feeling of love.

I do have reasons to rise above,
I can't stew on the ocean floor,
Others need me more,
I break to the surface once more.

The Sea Calls

The Sea calls to me,
On dark days,
When I miss the sun's rays,
Warm and kind.

When its cold as the sea,
I wish to bring out the sun's rays with me,
Let the rays dance on my skin like a wave coming to shore,
Waiting for the sun to rise once more.

Sea Floor to the Surface

Depression is like an anchor that only you can remove,
With the right help you can float from the sea floor,
Up onto the surface.

Anxiety is like a bee running rampant in your mind and stomach,
Only you can calm the bee,
Make the bee notice the flowers and honey.

Liberation from Depression

An anchor on my chest,
The ocean floor; I rest depressed,
Yet, if I and only I first.

Remove that anchor,
I'll float to the surface,
Steady and slow,
Gentle as the waves go.

I'll break to the surface,
Sun on my skin,
I find reasons to live within,
Count gratitude in the love I have.

It's okay to lean,
Let family and friends be your fence,
Sturdy and reassuring,
There for you to lean on.

Moods Like Seasons

You do not stew in moods,
Pull yourself out,
Love is what life is about!

Bitter winter might stay,
However, spring is fresh,
No need for a winters rest.

Autumn is cold yet,
If positivity takes ahold,
You'll feel the sun's gold.

Hurt

Pride and Stubbornness

Pride and stubbornness,
Can't win forgiveness,
Then you lost us.

What does it gain?
Loneliness and pain,
Look around; none surrounds.

Forgiveness is an open door,
For those I used to adore.

Hurt

Blood supposed to run thicker,
You hurt us,
So blind is time,
The past belongs there,
We're here in the present.

Where are you in our family?
You'll lose what you could see,
Therefore, no you and me.

Where are you in our family?
I see the sadness in your eyes,
We slipped through your fingers like sand.

Will pain be the thing you leave behind?
Its up to you both,
Phone number hasn't changed.

Not Second Best

We were not second best to them,
We are second best to both of you,
What did we do?

Blood splintered; us vs them,
You chose them over us,
We were never good enough.

We won't be second best to anyone,
You lost,
They won.

Separation

We were separated for our own good,
Memories only of loud voices shouting, and, crying,
Why must your pride blind?

Where was the love for us?
Pain, in place of where love should of grown,
You love them,
To you, they were more important,
We are of little worth to you.

We of little worth want to know you,
Only you can stop this hurting.

Sadness

The sadness of loss,
Hurting what was,
The hurting of us,
Must, we be so prideful?
It is your downfall.

The pain of separation,
The burden of misery,
Wondering, do you love us?
Weren't we worthy?
We're worthy in their eyes.

How can you despise?!
We were only young,
Only family left,
Does that not mean anything to you?

Longing

My Twin Flame

My Twin Flame,
You are my aim,
Your love I'll gain,
Make my heart aflame.

My Reason

You're my reason,
For why I'm still breathin'
You best be believin'
That my twin flame is my soul reason.

She

She is beautiful,
I am told,
I yearn to be the one she holds,
Promise, that our love will never fold,
Just to meet you; will be gold.

Knowing

I know about you,
You, know about me,
Though, psychically.
Isn't it funny?
Can't wait to meet you, honey.

I Want to Be

I want to be with my twin flame,
Without her is only loneliness and pain,
I want to be with my twin flame,
Golden, it will be to speak her name,
I want to be with my twin flame,
Thoughts, only of her on my brain,
I want to be with my twin flame.

I Wonder

I wonder about you,
What are you doing?
How was your day?
Are you okay?

I wonder about you,
Do you want and need me too?
Knowing you'll brighten my life,
Brightening and eradicating the darkness of my life,

I wonder about you,
I can't wait to meet you,
Know, I'm running to you.

My Word

I can only offer my word,
That you'll be my world,
Thoughts of you make my heart whirl,
Can't believe that someone like me,
Has someone like you waiting for me,
For the day where our hearts will beat in synchronicity.

Knight

I promise to be your knight,
I will fight for your dreams,
Repair your heart at the seams,
Defend your heart's desires,
For you will make my heart fire.

Queen

I'll treat you like a queen,
Respect and love you will redeem,
For, you'll be my heart's queen,
No one in between,
Only you in my dreams.

Fight

Fight for me,
Life can sometimes be tough you see,
Yet, use the thought of me,
To get you through the dark and stormy.

Like I use the thought of you,
To get me through life's gloom,
Only space for you in my hearts room,
No one else can get through.

Promise

I promise I'll respect you,
I promise I'll protect you,
I promise I'll laugh with you,
I promise I'll grow with you,
I promise I'll be the only one for you.

You

You will be my sun,
You will be my one,
You will be the goddess of my dreams,
You will be the one my heart deems worthy.

Sunshine on my Soul

Sunshine on my soul,
High vibration behold,
A love like gold.

Meant to be like destiny,
The path to get to me,
Is a test you see?

Please, leave that low vibration,
My tears drop with weight,
I am worth the wait.

Admiration

An Angel Appeared to Me

An Angel appeared to me,
With her light,
Showed me the right path,
With her care,
Taught me that I can love myself,
With her care,
Taught me that I can care about myself.

Oh, angel fair,
Do you know your effect?
Do you understand one's eternal gratitude?
How I love this angel so,
She is family.

Oh, angel,
You are sunshine personified,
Respected highly in my mind,
You'll remain on earth forever and,
Never age a day.

For YOU will ALWAYS be NEEDED and LOVED!
I wont let you get away.

Stay

Angel,
Dear to our hearts,
Not just for your gifts,
But for or your heart.

(I/ we) will do anything to see you happy,
(I/ we) promise to keep you forever,
Never go up on that cloud,
For (I/ we) want you around.

You are IMPORTANT!
You are LOVED!
You are a gift from ABOVE!
You give peace like a dove.

Do you understand,
If you do, then stay,
For forever and a day.

Joan

She is beautiful in mind, body, and, soul,
She is the queen of rock 'n' roll,
Joan made the stage equal for all.

Wear this poem like a badge of pride,
Take all of your accomplishments in your stride.
Tell them where to ride.

The way you sing is a beautiful thing,
Just like how you make that guitar sing,
Your talent is blinding.

Thank you, Joan, from my heart,
May your music and I never part,
For you made some of my ugly days art.

Stefani

Her beauty is of kindness,
Love (of/ for) her is timeless,
Love from her is the cure,
Her love is pure.

She has inspired many in the arts,
She has even touched my heart,
She saved me when I was in the dark,
To me she is pure art.

Her voice is like a best friend,
She is there with you till the end.

Good on her for preserving.
Stefani, you're deserving.

Thank you for being yourself,
You'll never know how much you've helped.

Chrissy

With the ferocity of a lioness, you battled illness.
Like a tigress you prowled the stage,
Leaving the audience caught in your gaze.

How many lives did you make aware?
Through your action and phrase?
Your strength does amaze.

You mastered your craft,
Your legacy is in your art,
Forever, in our hearts.

Mairi Mhor

Mairi Mhor,
I adore,
Wretched from your home,
Injustice with language shown,
Protested through tone,
Through, your singing alone.

Brave Scottish Flower

Brave Scottish flower,
Do you realise your power?
No one sits on a thistle,
They will get more than a prickle.

As your sting is like your fight,
Full of bravery and plight,
None in the world could sever,
My love for you and the heather.

Yellow Roses: Gia and Elyssa

Together through the thorns,
A pure love adorns,
Torn apart like a tragedy,

Golden as the sun,
Reflects their halos,
May these two roses rest.

Let them fly with angel wings,
For heaven, to them, sings.
Gia and Elyssa.

Poetess of Love and Life:
Natalie B

Poetry like blood flowed through your veins,
Amazon of 1900 your work still reigns,
Ahead of your time for it flowed to your will,
Like ink from a quill.

Your lovers came and went like seasons,
They were heaven sent,
You enjoyed the rhythm of life,
Natalie is the poetess of love and life.

For Whom Tarn Wrote

For whom Tarn wrote,
Was, for women like us,
Whom at sunrise; with lips pressed,
Whom at sunset; lips undone,
Read a verse to your lover.

As your words take over,
Tarn's beauty takes ahold,
Like a ghost; Tarn is here,
Holding your lover dear.

Reading your verse to break your curse?
For the dead live on from dusk to dawn,
Yes, why is Tarn gone?

Thoughts

A Note to those Clowns

Yes, you clowns,
Would rather see me down?
You won't ever come around?
See me now!

Yes, you clowns,
Take a look around,
I'm here and you're there,
I can live without a care!

Yes, you clowns,
No longer put downs,
I lift myself up,
You're missing my glow up!

Yes, this is a note to those clowns.

Kindness

Kindness is a gift,
Wrapped with care,
Giving for all to share,
Open that gift today!
Believe in a little sun ray!

Being kind is easy,
Kindness is breezy,
Hate is hard,
Like stones thrown by a heavy heart.

For kindness is in self-love,
Kindness is in self-care,
Kindness is a blessing,
Kindness is a cure to hate,
as it doesn't manipulate.

Ending of a Friendship

I am positivity,
You are negativity,
I see light,
You see dark.
Contrasts apart.

We end here,
I, to the future,
You, stuck,
I lifted you up,
You tore me down,
Emotions swirl around.

I lead with my heart,
You lead with your head,
You're so cynical and that's so typical.

One side: your's,
I sigh, letting go,
Saying goodbye is hard.

Yet,
I can finally see,
You were never there for me.

My friend,
Here we end.

Treatment

How do we treat each other?
Strangers that don't even bother,
It's not okay to be so abrupt,
Like interrupting a sentence suddenly.

Ghosting is a cowards game,
Like unfollowing an acquaintance,
Honesty should be the aim.

Lost Soul

Frustration with no direction,
Lost in a whirling dervish,
Feeling helpless.

Cries and screams
Of broken dreams,
What is the point?
O, life?
Why?!

When one asks for help,
All one gets is rejection,
Abdication of will,
Wanting out; screams throughout,

As the sun sets so does one's hope,
Slowly extinguished and finally,
Silenced!

Snake

Like a snake,
You slithered your way,
Into our fray.

Like a snake,
You left your sting,
Like a poison shaped ring.

Like a snake,
Splitting apart,
What matters at heart.

Like a snake,
You fooled your mate,
Your young not of his make.

Like a snake,
You slithered in another snake,
At what price are you willing to take?

Like a snake,
You may have shed your skin,
Yet, you know the wicked within.

Like a snake,
You are a bully,
That is you truly.

Nakama

My dear nakama you've taught me many things,
Like how friendship can give one wings,
Even to follow your dreams.

To never give up,
Even when it's tough,
To pick myself up by the gruff.

To believe in myself,
Anime and manga is the right stuff,
Thank you for getting me through the rough.

www.ingramcontent.com/pod-product-compliance
Lightning Source LLC
Chambersburg PA
CBHW021724190726
48289CB00008B/2676